CU00760238

DELTA GREEN

The Way It Went Down

Dennis Detwiller

ARC DREAM PUBLISHING • 2018

Delta Green: The Way It Went Down © 2018 Dennis Detwiller.
Introduction by Shane Ivey, © 2018. Published by arrangement with the
Delta Green Partnership. The intellectual property known as Delta Green
is ™ and © The Delta Green Partnership, who has licensed its use in this
volume. Quotations from other sources are © by their respective authors.
All rights reserved worldwide.

www.delta-green.com

Published February 2018 by Arc Dream Publishing
12215 Highway 11, Chelsea, AL 35043, USA

www.arcdream.com

ISBN 978-1-940410-36-4 (hardback)
ISBN 978-1-940410-35-7 (paperback)
ISBN 978-1-940410-34-0 (ebook)

Printed in the United States of America

Contents

Introduction
By Shane Ivey

DELTA GREEN, THE U.S. government's black project dedicated to stopping unnatural threats, has survived under one name or another for over ninety years. The individual stories that make up that long history never last very long. Its operations would be infamous for their desperation and high casualty rate, if anyone were to take the records public. If we are lucky, no one ever will.

In the meantime, Dennis Detwiller has written—reported? transcribed? channeled?—these moments from that hidden world. They're the shortest of stories, flickers of memory and glimpses of possible futures. There is no comfort to be found in their brevity. Horrors formed us, surround us, will subsume us.

But you probably know all that. When you learn about Delta Green, you either join the mission or you become the mission. You are already implicated.

SHANE IVEY
CHELSEA, ALABAMA
JANUARY 2018

The Key

OK. SURE. FIRST. OK. Listen. Innsmouth. It began in Innsmouth, Massachusetts in nineteen hundred and twenty-eight—write that down. It began there, but it didn't end there. Fuck. It's still going on. Right now. No doubt.

OK. Sure. You've heard rumors. That fucking silver hubcap in the desert in forty-whatever—true. The things the Nazis were calling at the bottom of the ocean? Also true. That city beneath the ice in the Antarctic. Fucking take three guesses. It's a big goddamn world, and we don't know shit.

How do I know? Me? I worked in this place. This was in the Fifties, so, you know, you wouldn't understand. We had our shit strapped down. We knew what was what. I was a file clerk. Just a kid who worked in a library and joined the Marines to fight some fucking Commies. Left in 1954, short about half my nerve. Got a job in Naval Intelligence because I pulled some geezer off the line and got him to a field hospital, and that guy—well, he was fucking connected. That job was just about heaven.

I'd file in the day and I'd file at night. "Do this, Don," and so, you know, I'd do it. Sometimes, I'd go in after hours to finish up and read. I read a lot of the files.

Then, one day my boss comes in the dry room where we keep all the old stuff. I'm filing. He's holding a fire axe. The axe looks like it's covered in Hershey's syrup, but I figure out right quick it's blood. I'm fast that way. He says to me, "Don." I say, "Yessir." He had the axe, right?

He says, "You want to know a secret?"

"OK."

He says, "Something owns us."

He holds the door for me, like, nice, and so I go. And when the door shuts, I hear him just open up. I mean, just screaming and smashing the shit out of everything. He was a smart guy, my boss. Not prone to violence. Not an unkind word in years. But he read everything. Every file that crossed that threshold. "Knowledge is power," he'd say to me. "Knowledge, Don, that's the key."

And he was fucking goddamn *right*. But a key to what?

The Junk Shop

I'VE SEEN TWO OF the books in twenty-two years. They came out of the Great Desert with some of the crazies who trek out there. I bought one for a week's worth of drinking at the Hole, the other for a '57 Packard. They're tin, the books, see? Only they're not. They look like tin but with green metal flecks in it, and the pages are metal—thin metal, like, with the writing burned into it.

They're big, the books. Oversized, but they don't weigh hardly nothing.

I read them now, every day. One is from a man named McCaw, who lived in 1651 in Shropshire, England. Had family myself there, back before we were all trundled off by Her Majesty to this glorious new continent. The book talks all old timey about England and a library and strange creatures and machines and stars and cycles.

The other book. Well, the other book is worse. It's from sometime after all this. Some Chinese world where they've taken over after some sort of atomic war or something. Heaven and hell, the books. With me in between.

These books, they're real. What's in them is real. I know that. I read them enough.

The first guy who brought one in to the junk shop, he set to drinking in the Hole, and he never did get out of that hole, if you know what I mean. He drove his truck into the river after telling me about the library out there in the waste. A library so big, and so filled with these books, that you wouldn't believe. A place that weren't built by no man. He marked it on my map.

I got my pack. I got food and water for days. I got my jeep and my rifle.

I'm going to go out to this library and see what else the books in the stacks have to say.

Into the West

WHEN THERE WAS NOWHERE left to go, I went west. Twenty-six days before, I saw my last road—nothing more than a dirt track, really—and I went past it, and up. Two mountains. A river so large I didn't think I'd be able to cross it. A field of yellowed grass as far as I could see. Now, here is here. And still the world goes west. My sat-phone stopped working somewhere before Rikaze and I threw it away. After all, I hadn't seen an outlet since Lhasa. I haven't eaten since the road, but I feel fine. The map said as much.

Seven years ago today, I received the book about the hidden plateau. It was written in 1903 by an Englishman whose name escapes me. A colonel in Nepal. Inside was a handwritten map with instructions. Go here, smoke this weed. Go here, drink from this stream. Sleep here, dream about the world. I did it all.

I should be in Kashmir by now, but I know I'm not. I know because at the second peak, the mountains stretched in all directions for as far as I could see. Endless. So I keep wandering west, certain I have slipped from the world of men forever.

Then, smoke on the far side of the valley.

The buildings there are clustered on the side of a mountain like goats gathered for warmth. The streets are empty, laid with rolling, perfectly colored stones. The sun is shining. I smell jasmine tea.

In the tea room, dozens cluster near to their ceramic cups, sipping. No one looks to me as I sit and tea is brought. Money is never spoken of, but I don't imagine the U.S. dollar would go very far here. I lose myself to the warmth of the tea, for awhile.

It is the first drink I have had in twenty-three days, but somehow it feels unnecessary.

The owner is a thin, prematurely old man with a wide smile. He goes table to table, pouring liquid and steam. At each, he stops and exchanges pleasantries in a language I can't identify.

"Abso elat, tende," he says to me, smiling. "Tende? Tende?" He pours more tea.

At the last table, the one farthest from me, he places the kettle on the wood, bows deeply from the hips, and mumbles something.

The figure there, covered in leather bib, is low and wide and in the dark. It stirs, and I think I see red hair. Then blue eyes. A white hand from beneath the dark leather waves the tea man off.

"Colonel," the tea man says, very clearly, and turns to the next table.

Inside

THE WILLIS TOWER HAS many, many rooms and I've been to all the real ones. Every day for the last twenty-four years, I've trudged the floors. I've worked all shifts. I've polished with machine and with my hands. I've wiped light switches and squeegeed miles of plexiglas. And every day for the last ten years, it's only "good morning Joe, how's your day?" followed by hours of silent cleaning, alone. Then home.

I'm a fixture here.

But then, I found the door. I opened the closet on 51, in the abandoned studio. The one with the stain that won't come out. Inside, I found the stage.

In the middle of a skyscraper, in the center, crossing down and through where the elevators should be, cutting through space where it could not be, was an old, unused stage. Victorian chairs overturned. Polished handles and old gas lamps. Cobwebs and scrawled graffiti.

Twice, in the rooms off that theater, I heard movement. Once, I saw a man. Or a shape. It skirted a wallpapered, wet hallway and turned the corner in a hurky-jerky way before vanishing. The rooms went on, and on, and on. But I was clever. I never lost my head, though I barely made it out. I ticked each wall with a grease pencil and followed the markings back to the door.

Now. Today. I have the food I need. I have the backpack. I have the flashlight.

It'll be "good morning Joe, how's your day?" and then I'll be in it. I'll be gone. To the place you can find only if you live in a place for long enough. A hole in the world where the rooms go on forever. And I'll find that man. And then I'll know.

I'll understand inside.

At the Shore

I NEVER ASKED WHERE greatgrandpop had been interred,
but he would talk about it from time to time. He said it was
a hot place, somewhere far from the sea. Far from Florida.
Greatgrandpop was 118 when he left, though we don't
tell anyone that.

"Why were you put there?" I asked him once,
when I was 9.

"You'll see, one day." He smiled and laughed.

Government men have come by twice in the time I've been
alive. I was very young. The first time, they sat at the kitchen
table with my parents and read some sort of legal docu-
ment to them. The second time, I listened outside the kitch-
enette window.

"—agreement of November 12, 1956, Frederick Gil-
man, prisoner #0201 YY Internment, Bellweaver, Arizona. In
exchange for certain items of national interest, the prisoner will
be remanded—"

On the night I found out, greatgrandpop whistled to me,
from the garage, his home.

"It's time, kiddo."

So I took him. A bundle of bones in a leather sac, neck
bloated, eyes bulging from whatever was killing him and we got
in the car. I had promised him. I promised. He didn't want to
die away from the sea.

We made the sea in less than ten minutes. I always feel alive
at the beach, even in the night. When his feet found the waves,

it was like he straightened. He shook off the blanket, and in the night I could see the sores all over his body. He turned and looked at me, wheezed, and smiled, and his teeth were flinty and small.

"Maggie, don't you follow me. Not yet. Start in the pool. Listen to your body. Go under. Wait."

And, faster than I thought possible, he disappeared into the surf. I thought I might cry, but I didn't.

Tomorrow will be the questions. For now, it's me in the pool, underneath. The water plugs my ears in a comforting way, like a hug, and I feel alone and warm and safe.

And in that silence, something speaks to me in his voice.

In the Back Seat

WHEN THE NEW AGENT dies, there isn't much to it. He curls in the back seat with his legs almost up to his chest, and he stops moving. We keep driving. There's nothing else to do. Everything smells of blood and then, after, everything smells like shit.

The smell reminds me of my son's birth, and why I have to do these things.

O'Hara weeps, though she didn't know him. No one did, really. Twenty hours earlier, the agent had been pecking away at a keyboard, safe in a safe as a cyberterror security advisor at some forgettable think-tank in Maryland. Then he was on our op.

Now, he is the mission.

We stop at the culvert off Long Lake, and I step from the car. I look around. The rest area is off season. Beneath the purple light of sodium arc lamps, snowflakes filter down. The gravel is covered in ice, and the lake is a black line at the edge of the trees.

I sat with my wife here in 1989 and roasted hot dogs and listened to the radio. We slept here and looked at the stars, before I knew the world was bullshit. Back when I was happy. Before I knew the stars looked back.

Tonight, I saw something like a dog made of swirling mirrors leap through the agent from a point in space that seemed somehow further than the edges of the room we were in. The agent staggered out with us when the freon fire-suppression system engaged, and we made it clear of the building before he sagged into my arms, covering me in blood from a thousand tiny holes.

I can't remember his name. It seems important now, at Long Lake, that I know his name. What his real name was, not the pseudonym we called him. But it won't come. This is not like me, and it disturbs me almost more than the body in the back seat.

It's not my first body.

I step to the trunk. Inside are two body bags, some garbage bags, chains, a hacksaw, an icepick, and four cinder blocks. I get to work.

My son is nine years old. I dreaded every day leading up to his arrival. I could say nothing to my wife. What could I say? How could I tell her? And then he arrived. Pure biological imperative in seven pounds, four ounces.

Adam. My unreasoning hope.

I open the back of the rental car and pull the agent out by an arm. The body slides out like a stillborn fetus and flops to the ground with a thud. In the cold air a wave of blood and shit fills my nostrils.

I think of Adam, and I know I have to get on with it.

Until it's someone else's turn.

Kay's Voice

'ANT'Į̦HNII — PRACTITIONER OF THE FRENZY Way.

Until May 2003, that was something from my Cultural Studies and Mores textbook, $199.95 at the University of Oklahoma bookstore (and Wonderwall was playing on the PA and it had snowed and my boots squeaked on the tiles... and...and...)

Enough. Okay. Start over.

Kay wanted to do it for her Ph.D. The ritual. The whole thing. She thought it would be great. She needed me, she said. To do it. She needed me to see. But it wasn't about that. It's hard to explain. I grew up with her, but we weren't real sisters; she was a cousin — lived with us. I worshipped her. I followed her to school. I followed her into cultural anthropology.

I followed.

"My doctors," dad would say, arms outstretched to hug us both. There, in that hug, I'd see Kay's eyes, green, watching me between strands of auburn hair. She knew.

Anyway, we went out to the woods to camp one night. Alone. I couldn't help myself. I loved her. I went willingly. Greedily.

Kay sang the huyachi song, the black song, and then she kissed me. We slept together. I wanted to. I had always wanted to. I always did. We slept together.

The next morning, Kay was gone. Then the search and the police and much later, the accusations. Nothing was ever found.

I mean, they found her clothes of course, because after the sing, she didn't need them anymore. I told them she was simply gone that morning. I didn't tell them about the dreams.

And here I am, 365 days later. Same night, same place. My father won't call me back. My family won't speak to me. And I'm here and I sing the song because I did it too. I broke the rules. I want to hear Kay's voice, again.

Finally, hours after the song is done. Footsepts beyond the light of the fire.

"Do not look at me," the voice says from somewhere off to the left. Is that Kay?

"Do not look..." another, smaller voice says from behind me.

"Come away from the fire..." the voice says.

"Come and see," the smaller voice says. Then...laughter? Moving in the dark.

I have come so far. I have seen so much.

I follow.

The Witness

I DON'T KNOW WHEN I came here, but it was a long time ago. This city is the greatest I have ever seen, and I have seen many, though my memory is dim.

I remember a time when I thought about such things. The why of everything. Why am I here? Who put me here? Why? Really, I no longer worry. Instead, I smile. There is no more why. There never was a why.

Sometimes it seems I'll go mad, waiting for so long. And I've been here a long time. A long, long time.

I'm the witness.

Extinction cannot occur without a witness.

Dear Cind

DEAR CIND,

I fucked up. What can I possibly write? How do I get it all across? I should've told you everything when it happened.

I should have said, what? Fuck. I don't know. This?

Hey Cind, how are you? A bunch of guys put these worms in themselves. They're not normal worms. They're from somewhere else. Okay, got it?

And these guys were robbing banks, and I was trying to find them. It was great. We had a map and everything. Phone records. Names. We followed them and photographed them and got ready for the raid.

And then one day, Cind, you won't believe this. One day I woke up naked, covered in vaseline, bleeding and sprawled at the bottom of an empty pool in an abandoned YWCA in Detroit. Remember the night of the twenty voicemails? Well, that's where I was, Cind. I wasn't dead, shot on some raid, I wasn't cheating. I didn't tell you then. I'm sorry. I lied.

So, here I am coming clean. These worms, they start out small. They crawl in your gut and grow, and they shit the philosopher's stone, and you live forever. Sounds great right? Only it's not. Only I've seen what's left of a body when these things are done with it. They breed and you explode like a party favor filled with rotting guts and flailing alien worms.

I've SEEN this.

There's a worm in me now.

I'm not going to wait around for it, and I see now, I can't write anything to you about it. I'm sorry, Cind. I'm so very sorry.

I love you.

The Phone Man and I

Don't see them anymore, I guess. Not that it matters.
And this was in, I don't know, 1990 or whatever? So, it was
like, a pay phone.

Fuck, okay, I'm old.

It was a specific pay phone at the time. You get me? A
little half-booth in the middle of the city. I won't say where. I
won't. It was invisible. No one even saw it anymore. No one
but me used it.

The first time he sent me there, it was to get instructions.
But get this, the phone never rings. I just stand there like a
shithead for ten minutes, and then eventually pick it up on the
voice, and it's already talking. And the voice is terse and bored
and sounds far, far away. "FRESH KILLS," it says, "190 Utility
Road, Fresh Kills, New York. Name, Donald Esbarger."

When I hung up — it was kind of an accident—I had
heard what I needed to hear, but he just kept on talking. So,
I, you know, do my job. It was like a million others. Nothing
special. And I get paid, and I go home, and I forget Donald
fucking Esbarger.

Only then, I wonder, did the guy on the line sit there all day
and all night? Did the phone-guy wait for someone to pick up?
No, because he was talking the whole time.

So I went back, and we had a chat, the phone-man and I.
We talked about a lot of things.

We talk about a lot of things.

The pay phones are gone, but the phone-man and I still talk, from time to time. He says the most marvelous things. He still knows how to crack me up. Even after all these years.

The Lady of the Rock

PEOPLE HAVE SEEN THE Lady of the Rock for maybe, what, eighty years? A hundred? A mermaid, a ghost. In our town, there were a thousand stories. Everyone knew about the ghost town—Innsmouth—though no one could agree just what had happened there. But the Lady was part of it.

The rock was a marker to the inlet. A scar of stone jutting from the sea like a rotted tooth. When I was a girl, I'd bicycle out to Abel Point and look at it, sometimes, scaring myself on the way home from municipal, thinking about her. Thinking about the Lady in the tunnels beneath that rock.

Thirty-two years later, I was crawling across that same rock in the rain, on the night of new moon.

Life can be strange sometimes.

I was looking for a carving on the stone. I didn't even know it was the same place until later. It didn't occur to me. I wasn't driving. It was dark.

You'll find, the more you deal with this stuff, the more these coincidences happen.

It was raining, and Albrecht was screaming from the boat, trying to train a bobbing light on the rocks. I found it, then, the mark, and took out the camera. Then the light fell on her.

She wasn't a mermaid, or a ghost. She was real. Above the waist, she was an old woman with bulbous black eyes, and an empty slot with hundreds of tiny, flinted teeth. Below the waist, just outside of the light, her hips shifted and exploded into a dozen flapping limbs which somehow supported her weight.

Her eyes found me, and her mouth turned up in a smile until it looked like it would connect with her eye sockets, and the center of her face would spill out. Like when you pop the top off of a Jack-O-Lantern and its guts spill out.

A finger like a chicken bone wrapped in sausage skin rose to her mouth. *Shhhhhh,* the gesture said.

We stood there for maybe ten seconds like that. Rain and Albrecht shouting. Then, I snapped a picture of the symbol, and ran back to boat.

You can see a part of her shadow in the picture.

And that's how I finally met the Lady of the Rock.

Are we done?

Between Here and Forever

I WAS BROUGHT IN as the science guy. "Ask the science guy," they'd say, never really engaging me until something needed to be looked at. But I was with them when they raided the lab.

I saw assets, they saw targets.

They didn't even glance at the notes on the whiteboard (covered in brains as it was). They didn't see the cryopreservation cylinder. They didn't pay any attention to me going through it all and picking up the notebooks. They didn't care. There was too much screaming. Too much arguing about what to do with the bodies.

I was the science guy; what else was I supposed to do?

I have a hot lab in my walk-up off Gramercy Park. It wasn't that hard to make. Negative air pressure and a scrubber and everything. I've been working on what I found in that lab for the last four months.

Ivan is a Wistar rat. He's the first subject of the new virus, drawn from that anonymous lab with its $750,000 particle scrubber below a Pet Smart in Brooklyn, and he's extremely healthy. Now.

After the first injection, he spent thirty hours twitching on the cage floor, and then went through an hour and half of convulsions. After that he vomited up his stomach, esophagus, other things. I still have them in a freezer somewhere. I was more interested in his blood. Because after that, after he chewed off his own esophagus, he was fine.

He hasn't eaten in twenty-two days. He hasn't defecated anything but the rotting remnants of his intestines, and he has not urinated at all.

Ivan doesn't eat anymore.

Yet, there he goes, crawling across my hand like he had all the time in the world. And I think he does. I'm pretty sure he does.

It Was Not Her

IT WAS NOT HER, again.

I have been doing this for longer than I have known what it is I am doing, but everything I have done has been working towards a singular goal. Does that make sense? It sounds strange out loud. I want to be clear.

The first one I did appeared at the time to be without any reason. Looking back now, the path is evident.

I read a book about plane crashes once. When you approach a crash, you see small things first. The plane sometimes hits and scatters debris or explodes in the air and tumbles in. But there is always a core, always some center. The main point of impact.

That is where I am now, and looking out at the spray of corpses, I can see the reasons arcing backwards in time to claim those poor innocent people, projected from where I am now.

They all had to die, even if I did not know why, then.

Of course, now it is no problem at all to look for her. I rather enjoy it. I look forward to it. And even though this was not her, again, I know sometime soon that HE will lead me to her. That I will find her. That I will free her and then be taken into *his* church.

Do not worry for me. I have faith.

Words

PEOPLE THROW THE WRITTEN word around like it is less than garbage. Like it is worthless.

Words can kill, my dear. Symbols twice over. They can teach others to kill. They're more dangerous than speech, though speech has its purposes. You can bury words, you can print them on a million sheets, you can tattoo them on your skin.

Writing was created to cut open this world. That's the whole reason for it. What do they teach, that the first civilized man appeared in Mesopotamia ten thousand years ago? Do you truck with such nonsense? Pity.

You really should know mankind had already come and gone and come and gone many times before this cycle.

We learned the written word from the others during the last one. It was a trap of course. Something that came to us in dreams. Write something down. Perfect the shape and unravel the world.

There is a symbol that makes fear, just like there's a shape of a line that can cut through steel and there is an oval that makes people go insane and a series of intercut lines that put you on the path to total control; that can pop a hole through and let you see forever. I've learned them all. It's taken time. But they work.

I hired a guy, this guy with a etching machine, to cut the symbol into a pendant for me. He'll see the symbol, but he won't understand it. It takes years. He won't LIVE with it.

But I'll wear it. I'll use it.

And I'll see what I can see. I'll see what the words were made to do.

End of the World of the End

THE PARTIES STARTED SOMETIME in the last five years, though it's hard to remember when I first heard about them. Small at first. Mini-Burning Mans, sprouting up like weeds at the edges of towns and cities. People drunk and drinking and later fucking, and then shooting. And then the police.

Later, the army.

It was a puff-piece. Something on the news, and then, on some cable program. People chatting in front of a sea of drunks. People would just up and leave their lives. Some went to see what it was like, and didn't come back. You got sucked in, somehow, though no one ever talked about it. The media never let on something strange was at work. It was just another stupid fad, like hippies, like legal pot, like raves.

Then one day, you woke up and they were a thing. Revels. On the news. Police blotters. SWAT team plans. Riot police moving in and spraying down 10,000 people outside Akron, Ohio, with tear gas and rubber bullets. The count topped 2,136 dead by the time they stopped doing the news. No one cared. It was over, somehow. There was no struggle. The world abandoned itself.

They stopped everything, the revels. It just took some time. It needed to get up to speed.

The strange thing was that the revels weren't about young people. The young people, for the most part, stayed away. It was the old people. Sometimes the really old people. Out there in the dark around a bonfire, nearly naked, holding a .38 pistol and calling someone a motherfucker.

I was there. I saw one up close.

We had to pass through it to get here, to get north and away. Boston burned, and by that point, I had shot someone, but law was no longer my main concern. We drifted through the party that ate up I-93. Cars on fire. People walking around, drunk, stumbling. Shooting. I saw two men in their fifties, with beer guts, struggle and grunt on the ground, and I couldn't tell if they were fighting or fucking, in the dark.

I lost my group there, as the crowd closed in. We had quit Manhattan University seven days before, and marched north, to make it to my family's summer house in Vermont.

My dad called me nine days before, and shot my mom, and then himself, on the phone, while I listened. Did I say that already? Am I repeating myself? I'm sorry.

The old woman grabbed me, and pulled me close to the fire, and I almost fell in. It stank of plastic and ruin, the burning car, and I stumbled at its edge before catching my balance. She smiled at me, and her teeth glowed green-blue in the light. The debris in the fire clicked and clacked at my feet and kicked up sparks as I wobbled forward.

They were bones. Human bones. Children's bones. Black and ash covered, in the fire. Oh, I ran. I ran away. I didn't look back.

And here I am, now, at the end of the world. A revel for all time. One last rager before the party's over, forever. Stay with me? There's a fire.

What the Voice Said

INSTRUCTIONS: OPEN MIKE IN a sound proofed room. Studio. Nothing chintzy. If you're feeling paranoid, kill the line with a diode. Close it off. Hit record. At night. Ask questions. Talk. Talk to the air. Then, listen to that tape. Turn the gain all the way up. Headphones on. Listen.

Listen.

The first time, I did it to kill the time. To test the wiring on the new board. Ten minutes maybe. "Test one two, one two, who are you..."

Two months later I found it. The tape. Dug it out and ran it and wondered what was on it (I never labeled it). Put it on and pushed the system. "TEST ONE TWO, ONE TWO, WHO ARE YOU..." boomed my voice from the speakers, followed by a hiss, and then, just as my finger found the STOP, the voice, there, in the back, stealthy. Quiet.

"I am."

A child's voice. A whisper. Like someone in the corner of the empty studio, far from the mike. It was a voice with a sly smile in it. Far, far, away.

I left then, walked that fucker off. Smoked a smoke. Said hey to the night guy. Came back with a coffee and ran it again. Same thing.

This time, I let it run, all 10. The voice was there again, after mine, then the hiss of air banging together like billiards. Then, at 9:53:09, again, the voice, closer now.

"They're coming." CLICK.

I ran it again.

The next week I was leaving work at 6:50 AM when a woman came out from behind the cement pylon and produced a badge. DEA, it read, Agent Grant. Was I Malcolm Steyr? Did I once work with a man named Reily at the Chicago PD to examine the answering machine tape of a murder victim. Sure, I said, how was Reily?

Dead, she said.

"Don't trust them," the little girl told me, later, when I asked her what it meant.

"Grant is not her name," she told me.

The tape ran and ran.

Now, we're in a car, driving in the black towards something I don't fully understand, but she's told me enough. The two in the front keep their eyes on the road ahead, on the dirt track taking us out into scrub country. My headphones in, I listen to the track, as the voice narrates what we're doing, what is coming before it's here.

The gun is a lump of warm metal, hidden in my lap like a promise.

Water Town

THERE ARE ENTIRE TOWNS under water, there since the Thirties, down, drowned, in the dark. I grew up on the lake next to one and never knew it. Grandy told me, out at his trailer, after his fourth bottle was chucked and smashed at the tin wall covered in chicken wire. About Danvers and the Donnels, and the devil.

Danvers Lake was called Danvers, Arkansas, back in the day. Then the WPA showed up and blocked the Tuft river with the dam. The Donnels ran booze, and guns before that and had a bunch of money stashed in the town. Gold. Silver. That was the rumor. Anyhow, the sheriff buddied up with the Feds and ripped up a bunch of the town as it was evacuated, all the while waiting to scoop up the Donnels if they showed. They didn't. And the sheriff didn't find shit.

The town flooded, treasure and all.

Before the war, Tommy Donnel drowned out there, in the lake, looking for his gold. His brother Taft quit the town and joined up and spent three years in some Pacific hellhole. He came back and built a shack out on the lake. I grew up looking at that tar shack from my window. I'd see the man who lived there from time to time. Strange. Big and gangly and without age. Bald and slick like a seal.

He'd swim out there in the lake, and dive. I remember this clearly. He'd dive and not come up for minutes. Always in the same place. Straight across from my house. Gold down there in the dark, waiting.

Once Taft Donnel shook his fist at my dad when he was a boy, and Grandy went out there with a shotgun and had words. Grandy says Donnel lost it in the Pacific. That he was soft. Donnel told him the devil was named "Tulu" and that his time was at hand. Nothing could stop the devil who would work his ways on him.

Taft Donnel died like he lived, drinking paint thinner. Years later, when I was like, ten, they found him. The county buried him. His shack was knocked flat by Moe's pickup truck and dragged off. No great loss.

I dream now about spires and doorways and empty windows alive with fish. Of murky water floating in what were once kitchens. Winding staircases that lead up to, but never reach, open air. Green waving plants growing from the peaks of roofs like waving hands, barely touched by dim green light. Walls and boxes and safes, filled with gold in the black.

I can hold my breath a long time now.

The Last Machines

IN THE VOID, THERE is no time. Systems turn, and connect, and after that, emergence into...chaos. Returning, we find a ruin bloated with the animal filth of the former age, grown and spread and madly overcertain of its position as master. Once, they worshipped us as gods. Once, we showed them the stars and the secrets of the angles and communion with the powers, both above and below.

Once, we fed on them and they were glad to be of use.

Now, they fashion crude sticks of metal into weapons they imagine more effective than flint and sinew. They fumble at the locks of eternity and steal an ember from beyond that might excise an entire disgusting settlement from this hollow world, and they imagine themselves clever. They are animals blindly reaching beyond the veil to grab hold of whatever knowledge they can, waving it about like some flame to ward off the dark. If they grab at the wrong thing, we will all burn.

It has gone too far, and we are too few, now. Ruin came. The order fell, and then, lesser orders, each more imperfect than the one before it, faint echoes of that vast and perfect time, when we alone were in control.

To wake, now, in this place is an omen. Those who came and fell before us, those imperfect few who survived our damnation fell. They fell to the apes, they fell to the thirst for blood, they fell to petty conflicts with others of their kind. They fell because they were impure.

We alone are the last of the line. Ascendant when the giants walked, and still clutching to power when the last, ragged outpost of our kind fell to internal ruin, our line will rule again. There are secrets buried still, lost in the deserts, forgotten in places where man cannot go.

Our illusion is perfect. We walk unseen through their streets, in the child's scrawl of their world before us, and we resist the call to feed. The smells. The meat. We resist, for there is clarity in starvation, just as in our disguises, there is freedom among the savages.

And then, in the desert, where we buried our last machines, there is salvation.

Life in a Box

WE WENT OUT IN the desert, after the old man told me where to go. The group called me, and he was the one that showed up, and that was good enough for me. In a parking lot at a Cash & Carry, he got out of his old T-Bird, and stepped to my car.

He was old, but alive, and packing. His face was steroid-fat, but it didn't carry down to his body, which looked like a picked clean skeleton. The smell hit me when he settled in, and brought back memories of my mom. Chemotherapy.

We drove for a long time.

The site was new. Some energy concern was putting up a grid of huge, lumbering fans in the middle of the desert outside of Inland Empire. Things the size of high-rises. A place no one ever thought they'd put anything. Yet here it was: a pilot site for a huge complex, hundreds of millions of dollars, thousands of eyes and hands working the ground every day.

The old man had buried something there, a long time ago. Something the group didn't want found.

We arrived at dusk, and tooled around for fifty minutes, lights on for the last twenty, looking. Finally, with a grunt, he signaled we should stop. There, at the edge of boulders the size of houses that the earth had spat out a hundred million years before Inland Empire, was a capped, small well.

We got the shovels and went over. The old man considered the well. One white stone, the size of a brick, pointed to the southwest.

"There," was all he said, pointing about five feet out from the well on the side of the rock. I told him to sit. I told him I'd dig. He sat, which was good. It took a long time. When I finally struck the box, it let out a hollow booming sound. It was only a foot or two down, but the ground was hard.

"Get out of the hole," the old man said, and I did. That's when I heard a noise from the hole.

The box was something like a PVC coffin. Pearlescent plastic of green and light green. On its lid was a scraped sigil. Something like an eye, or a flame, or a tree. Dirt slid in the cuts on the surface, coloring them red.

"Carl? Carl is that you?" The voice from the box said, muffled, but clear. Then, a stream of panicked words.

"Don't listen to it," the old man said, and pulled out a cylinder from his pocket. An old-looking incendiary grenade.

Inside the box, the thing begged us to let it out.

"Get the kerosene. I should have done this a long time ago." He gave me an apologetic shrug.

Where the Trains Don't Go

I TOOK THE TRAIN uptown, got off, and walked. I went on to where the trains don't go, to see for myself. A ruin of fallen brick and collapsed roofs. Empty, trash-strewn streets. Chainlink fences boxing the world, lazily collapsing over years. Decades.

There's nothing up there. Nothing left. Empty store windows. Furtive shouts. A dog, out there, where the world ends.

The book talks about this. How the great city will turn and digest itself, like the oroborous, the snake that eats its own tail. On page 26, it outlines the chants and incantations, and the places to do them. To call them. From outside.

On the TV, the talk is of missiles and Congress, and tanks on some Czech horizon on the other side of our little planet, triggers straining. We will all die in a conflagration which makes their war look like a fireworks show. A war no one knows about. A war we're all living.

Still. One must carry on. I go where the trains don't go, anymore, and do my work. Quietly. Quickly. Cleanly.

"Kid. You want twenty bucks?"

His eyes are liquid and shining. His face, freckled. There's self-preservation in his stance, ready to turn, ready to run off to some shit hole in this no man's land. But then he steps towards me, furtively. Greedily.

We cross to the building without a roof, my makeshift open air cathedral, and no doubt he thinks my needs are more simple. More base.

First, he sees the symbol. Then, he sees the skulls.

He never sees the knife.

The Last Go Round

HE WAS SMILING WHEN I shot him in the face. A neat little black gap appeared just over his mouth but beneath his nose, like a hole poked through a mask, and his head spat out a gout of red and pink all over the wall behind him. It slid down the bricks like a slug. This all seemed to happen very, very slowly.

He slid a little bit to the side, head drooping, eyes open but glazed, but he didn't fall. It was over.

I felt the movement of air and turned to find the coffee house suddenly empty of customers. The pistol looked huge, comedic almost, smoking in my hand. I spun, waving it around, shouting.

The woman behind the counter had covered her ears, fingers lost in dreadlocks, and then dropped out of sight. I shouted things I couldn't hear because my ears were shrieking. Don't move, I think I said, don't look.

I crouched and snatched up the doll which had dropped to the ground from his dead hand. It was rough-made. Straw with pineyes and a ragged jacket. A straw woman in a sport coat, as made by a poor child in some third-world hellhole. A little sport coat made of tan suede.

Just like the patch I found missing from my tan suede jacket last month, when the dreams began.

Have you ever dreamed about killing, skinning, and eating your child? Because I have. I've dreamed it every day since that break-in. I dream it whenever I close my eyes.

I lifted the barrel and shot him one more time, and the empty meat jumped. The body slid out of the booth, wiggling, and flopped to the ground.

"FUCK YOU," I yelled, and heard only the bass in my head over the tinny shriek of the gunfire.

I wiped my mouth with my sleeve, smelling gunpowder, and was suddenly stung by something small and hard spattering my face. A pock-marked hole had appeared in the brick wall kicking up dust. Then another one. Higher, small and circular, with the curly cue of a cloud of dust swirling from it.

Then I heard CLAP CLAP CLAP. Little faraway sounds.

The cop looked like a pop-up target, hunched in the door, pistol out in front of him smoking and spitting a lick of flame with each shot.

I shot the window above his head and it exploded and the fat cop stumbled backwards out the door and fell to the ground outside.

"I DON'T WANT TO KILL YOU!" I screamed, and then moved through the back of the kitchen before a terrible thought struck me. I froze, gun dangling, looking at some stupid hippy shit in the sink.

What if the dreams don't stop? What if. What if. What—

Group

PEOPLE WALK AROUND BAREFOOT here, because there's really nowhere to go, and they keep it warm, or the desert does, whatever. It's warm here and people don't wear shoes. God.

Why is everything so fucking hard all the time?

It's been nine days since I said the name out loud, which, all told, is pretty good. I'm impressed with myself. The last time Sebastian was here, he told me the group was paying attention and had someone on the inside. They were paying my way, after all. Someone was transcribing my therapy just as, a few days later, some other someones were reading it in Washington. A weekly play by play. Will the security risk crack? Tune in and find out.

Of course, there's always the chance this is all in my mind. The group. The op. The corpse sitting up on the table and talking. The screaming. My screaming.

Let's face it. It would be really nice if I were only losing my mind. I don't think that's what's happening. I just can't get behind that. That's not what's happening.

I think I saw a man run from the inside like a reverse puppet. Something had squirmed inside him and inflated him, stretching his skin to splitting until it looked like naugahyde left out to burn beneath a supernova. Pale blue white with horrible red cracks that ran like seams across his limbs.

"Yasmine?" the doctor looked at me like a mechanic looks at a faulty engine, disassembling me in his mind. Doctor Douchenozzle Gajar, puzzle man.

My face settled into smile number six; a calm, recollection filled smirk. In my mind, I saw the puppet thing shake twice and then split down the middle like a faulty shopping bag, spewing a web of undulating eels and liquid the color of antifreeze. Monty just sat there crying. For a bit. I mean, then, it fell on him.

I burned down the L.A. County morgue. I can say that now. It's no exaggeration. I lit the autopsy room first. Shot at a deputy when he came in, and then walked room to room starting relatively awful fires with rubbing alcohol and embalming fluid. Didn't kill anyone. Well, no one real. Almost got a fire guy, though, but he got out.

All the fucking worms were harmed in the making of this program, though. Good, right?

"Do you have anything to add today?"

It just comes out.

"I didn't catch that," he takes his glasses off, holding the bridge of his nose.

I swat the glasses from his hands and stand up, laughing, my hand numb. He looks at his empty hands, and sighs. This doesn't even phase him. I need to phase him.

"I WANT TO TALK ABOUT THE WORM!"

Doctor Gajar spins his finger in the air and the orderlies are in the room.

"FUCK YOU, FUCK! THE WORM THAT WALKS! THERE'S A WORM THAT—"

Face Games

WHEN WE FIRST STARTED wearing the mask, it was a small thing. Something between two friends. Hell, more than friends. Whatever. We loved each other. But it was a joke. Something funny you did. Put the mask on, stalk around the house not speaking to the other. Do the laundry in it. Take a shower. Silent.

Where did the mask come from? I couldn't tell you now, and I didn't start asking that until after. When it showed up, it was something humorous though. Something goofy. Fun. Something to take the edge off.

We weren't supposed to be seeing each other, you see, though A-cell knew. Anyway, when it slipped off the cogs, everything fell to shit very quickly. Why else would I be here, right? Lucky to be alive. Yup.

There was a time when she tied me up, while wearing the mask. Tied me up and made me lie there on the floor while she paced, naked, with a knife. I'm not going to lie; I liked it. I thought it was great, until the first cut.

Three hundred and forty stitches and nine hours of surgery later, here I am, alive. She's gone. They found the mask, though, in a sewer pipe a mile from the house. So that's good, right? Maybe I'll see her again, huh? Maybe she's somewhere in it still.

My face is almost there, they say. Soon. Soon it'll be close to normal. But it'll never as smooth as that mask.

There's Life Underground

IT IS LONELY, UNDERGROUND. Sometimes, I call to people above and bring them down, here, to where I live.

We talk. They tell me of the world above. When we are through, they live on, within me.

The book is what did it, I think. That damnable book I found on Bleecker. I read it, and it did things to me. It changed me. The walls of the apartment were white, and soon, so was I. First my nails, then my limbs. Then, my face. Finally, my pupils. In the mirror I cracked (the mirror from Belfast that told me things), I was a shadow of white, on that last night I slept above the street.

I had to eat.

First, birds. Then cats and dogs. Finally a horse. Almost, once, a child. All after the sun went down, In the dark.

This was a long time ago. I am in control of my appetites now, but then, I was nothing more than a ravenous animal. But I have grown into my own.

When I first heard the singing, at night, from the drains, I thought (prayed) I had finally gone mad.

But New York City is alive on all levels. Things walk the streets just as they walk beneath them. They are friends now. Friends. There is Abraham, and Johann, and Markus, and Emma.

We sing at night in the tunnels and eat, together. And they tell me of another world beyond this one, a world of dreams. But, they say, I am too young. Too inexperienced to find the tunnels through. Someday. Someday. They smile and show me their teeth.

We eat a great deal, you see.

It is not so different here. Even the immortal dream of an afterlife.

What's Your Name?

I HAD BEEN TREATING her for ten months when I realized whatever was in her, was mocking me. It was never obvious. It never went out of its way to do it. It just demonstrated through conversation that it was entertaining itself with me. I was simply a sparring partner, never a threat.

She was 11 years old when I began treating her. It was the day after her birthday. Head injury, catatonic stupor. All pretty standard.

Four months in, I realized she was still conscious somewhere in that still body—back when I thought there was a "her." Five months and I had my first successes with hypnosis. Eight months and I was certain I was on my way towards something significant, maybe a new type of treatment. And then, I realized, all at once, that what was in her was not her. This girl was gone. There was something else.

Now, when we talk, it is an interrogation.

"When will you tell me who you are?"

"Soon."

"Tell me something. Prove to me you are from somewhere else, like you say."

"The city of New York is a ruin, filled with corpses."

"No. No, it's not."

Then, that smile. The smile again. The one you should never see on a child's face.

"Wait."

Four weeks ago, it told me to invest in gold, and I did. I don't know why, but I did. I made a lot of money. A great deal of money. I wipe my lips, trying not to show my fear.

"What's your name?"

"Abd al-Hazrad."

Something Behind the Eyes

I FOUND THE INCONSISTENCY, first, in a duplicate record. Something stuck to the back of a file folder in the stacks. Personnel files and from the 1970's — maybe earlier. That's when this all started. That was eight months ago.

She says her name is Mary Hettu, but I know that's not true now, it was one of the first things I uncovered. Mary Hettu died in a house fire in 1975 in Burke, Michigan, the week of her ninth birthday. She was black.

I had enough to expose her then, but I went deeper. Her fingerprints came back as Talia Esiet, native of Malta, born 6/6/22. Once the thread was out, I kept pulling on it, to see how far it could unravel. How long until it all fell apart revealing...what?

I confronted her with the picture I dug up on Esiet, a grainy black and white of an old lady standing on some Mediterranean beach, squinting. "Mary" looked at me, and there was something sad, something behind her eyes that made me disengage.

We've been together for a long time now, "Mary" and I, Since that night really.

I've been noticing things. Bad things, and it means either I have slipped or there's something about Mary Hettu I haven't yet uncovered. I'm three lifetimes back in her history, and I'm beginning to think this isn't some sort of con. Yet, I find myself attracted to her power. Something is wrong though, I know that, I'm not stupid.

This morning, after she left for instance, there were reptilian scales the size of quarters in my sink.

What Do You Do?

WHAT DO YOU DO for a living? It's a boring question, yet it's asked all the time.

There are two answers to this question.

There is the party answer: I am a defense consultant for the government.

And then there is actual answer: I sit in an office in Maryland and read books or watch television. Occasionally, there is a wrong number. Otherwise, the office is silent. Twice a month, a healthy paycheck is dropped in my account.

I have no boss. No one to report to. Nothing. How did I get such a marvelous job? I had the foresight to copy everything when I worked at Sandia labs. I understood what we were working on to a point, and that point was this: it was going to kill a lot of people, someday. That's all I really needed to know. But I saw other things, too.

I saw a small, handheld, box-shaped object flatten a target radiosonde at four miles with no apparent projectile, like it projected an invisible beam of force ahead of it. There was no power source.

I wasn't supposed to be at the range that day, but I came in to get my jacket and keys and I watched it along with the group. "What are we looking at?" I asked, and my boss looked at me and smiled and laughed and said "That's nothing."

I was always a saver. I was always about contingencies.

When I rolled out the plan to my former boss, he listened, his face and mood darkening. It is to his credit that he said only one thing to my proposal: "We can come to an arrangement."

We did. This is year four of our arrangement. I have not spoken to him since leaving the labs.

I miss it sometimes, here, in my bubble.

White Was Coming In From the Edges

THERE ARE A THOUSAND books about the end of the world.
A thousand movies. Mad Max. Whatever. It's a moment you
never think you'll end up at. You never think about it like a
place you will go. You never think, Oh, yeah, finally, here we
are everyone. Welcome. Welcome.

You never think you'll *cause* the end of the world.

In any case, you never think, If I shoot this kid, it'll end the
world. Is that a normal thought? Does it make sense? I never
thought it. I didn't know. That's all I can really say. I really had
no idea and I'm really very sorry, okay? Get off my back. It was
just another op. Just another fucking night at the opera.

The kid jumped on Gwendolyn and her SIG Sauer went
off twice, taking out the window. But she was dead before she
hit the floor. The kid was naked. Blue-skinned. Its face and hair
were pitch black, slick with blood. The eyes were rings of silver.
The teeth were split and blackened, sprawling and yellow. I say
"kid" because we had known him before all this.

Gil had said the spirit was trapped in him. The kid was a
door. The Inlut-Shua. The Wendigo. It was trapped. But we all
knew I wasn't going to let this little shit rip my throat out. If I
don't sound too upset about Gwen, let's just say she could have
learned not to drop her gun, but she and the kid had history.
Whatever. She wasn't worrying about anything anymore.

She was safe, finally.

So, I shot the kid. Ooooh. I know. I put one through his chest and it was like someone threw a bucket of oil out of his back. But still, he crossed the fifteen or so feet to my face so fast that there was only a second shot before his hands would be on me.

I saw a silver eye swing in front of the gun sight, out of focus, and I closed my eyes and emptied the gun. I fell to the ground and landed half in and half out of the farm house. Upstate New York. Summer.

The snow began to come down.

I ran back to the car. I didn't even check on Gwendolyn. Didn't matter, no one was there. She was dead, I'm sure. It didn't matter. By the time I was on the highway, it was a blizzard. Snow everywhere in July. Drifts piling near overpasses. Wind whipping curling patterns in the freezing air.

No cars. The clack of my tires catching the ice, windshield wipers keeping time as I crawled east.

There were parked cars, but nothing running on the road. Just me. Lights worked. The radio: static. Nothing. No people.

I hit the city and turned up Memorial, and the snow was still coming down. White was coming in from the edges. I stumbled from the car and began moving up to the apartment on foot. Slipping on the ice in the empty city. A tomb.

I had not seen a single person.

And I heard it, then, in the distance, a howl that tracked down the street with a hollow ring. A song for me, alone.

I turned on the street and the wind caught me full-on, making my eyes water.

I stumbled and began to run.

The Strange People

I CAN SEE THEM, and I think I know why no one else can.

They stand out to me. They feel different, even though they somehow look the same. Each one is carefully nondescript. None share the same characteristics except maybe a flatness to their eyes: a look that says, "I will consider you with equal import as the wall, or the door, or the car; you are a thing to be catalogued." I call them the strange people.

Anyway, no one else sees them, and it's because of the accident.

For nineteen days when I was twenty-two, I was unconscious. It wasn't like the movies told you. It wasn't the record skip of a coma, or some portal to the afterlife. I dreamt I was like a slug in some vast, stone room. But that's not right. I was a slug. This was not some vague feeling. The dream held the certainty of reality that the best dreams hold. Only I didn't want it to hold that, you know? I didn't want it to be real. So it's not.

Sometimes, I can think about it in a way where it's not a dream and it's still all right. But most of the time, if I do that, things get bad.

So. The dream.

In the dream, I crept and stared. Somehow I swung my point of view to great heights above my body. I hummed. I hummed like the air being let through an old car horn. Like a fat man sitting on crushed bagpipes. I slid and stretched, leaving a trail behind like an oil slick.

My hands weren't hands. They were clackers. Blue.

Like a lobster or something. Ha.

Don't you think I know how it sounds?

The world beyond the room was indistinct, lit green and red. My skin tasted the wind, and it was ripe with rotten meat, rotting plants, and the sea.

There were books, too. Someone...told me they were books, anyway. Metal books. At first, some of the others there tried to get me to do things. Things with the books. But after a time, they left me alone. They said nothing, but I knew they thought there was something wrong with me.

Hysterical. I know.

When I woke, I spent seven months in rehab trying to forget the slug-dream. It was an ischemic attack, they said, or a minor stroke. I was lucky, they said. I would make a nearly full recovery, in time.

I was a slug, I said.

People smiled and laughed uncomfortably. I learned not to say anything about it after the prescriptions came. I ditch the pills, now. They interfere with the machines.

I built my first machine a week after moving into the new apartment. I'm not sure how, but it makes things slow. Whatever. It was a broken toaster oven, a remote control, and an iPad with a smashed screen. Now it's useful. I dropped a Snickers wrapper above the machine when I first built it, what? Two years ago? It's still falling.

I just know things, too. Like how the Ukraine thing went. Yeah, I knew he was going to get killed, and then the bomb.

I knew all about that. So much, that when I told Jenna how it was going to go, and she laughed me off, that was the last I ever heard from her.

Only now, the people are here. I see the people because they were there with me in the slug-dream. They're here now to fix me—the mistake. But I've been building a lot of machines.

I've been buying a lot of gear and making the shapes I can see in my head when I close my eyes. They do things. They make things happen.

When they finally try and come for me, they'll get a nasty surprise.

The Weight of
the Water

THE ATTACKS BEGAN ON 4/22/16 at Prince and Greene Street at
10:45 P.M. The first victim was a teenager, Javier M. Calhoun,
male, 13 YOA. The boy was walking back from the Genovese
drug store and "something fell on him" from an overhang. Wit-
nesses saw the boy run into traffic with something dark on his
back. He was struck by an Uber SUV, then taken to Mt. Sinai
via ambulance, where he briefly regained consciousness. He
claimed to have been attacked by an animal approximately the
size of a raccoon, with "human teeth."

Bite marks on Calhoun's neck match this assertion.

Calhoun died later that night from internal injuries.

Oddities. Calhoun was missing his right eye, even though
he was not struck by the vehicle in that location. Claw marks
indicate something pulled the eye out of his head. The boy's
testimony was poorly recorded on a cellphone and was
nearly incoherent. Calhoun claimed the animal was saying
something to him.

Two blocks away at West Broadway, 6/12/16, 8:22 P.M.
Next victim, Aaron S. Webster, 4 MOA. An infant. Mother
was in the living room of a two-bedroom apartment folding
laundry within fifteen feet of the child. Warm night. Windows
were open. Boy was asleep in a child carrier on bed. Suddenly the door to the bedroom slammed. "But there was no
one there," the mother claims. A moment later, as the mother
rushed to the door, the door was locked from the inside. By the

time the mother smashed the door down, the baby was gone. Left behind on the bed were three split human finger bones, the marrow scraped out. The mother was sedated and has been voluntarily committed to the Manhattan Psychiatric Center.

Child was never found. Scraps resembling child's clothing recovered near a water outlet pipe at Franklin Street Station (fluid typing was a match).

West Broadway and White Street, 9/10/16, 9:05 P.M. Fifth Precinct Officer Patsy Sherburne responds to a call for assistance at the corner. There, 1st Precinct Officer Dwight Marcovich is attempting to remove Evan S. Burke, 66 YOA—a known indigent—from a sewer opening. The man is caught, legs in a sewer hole. He is screaming. Much of this is captured on video.

When the officers pull him clear, most of his lower legs are gone. He bleeds out before the first ambulance arrives. Marcovich fires several shots into the open manhole. Sherburne reports "dozens of human eyes looking back" at her from the dark.

We respond, 10/02/16, 6:54 A.M. It is reported as a water main burst, and technically, it is. We just never mention we're the ones who caused it. Four train stations are shut down, and because we hold off the repair crews (calling in a few favors), the water rises as high as your ankles. It covers six blocks for ten hours. That was Abby's idea. "Let's see if they can swim," she said. We already knew they only went out at night.

Two days later, the first specimen comes in. Recovered by Animal Control and Welfare, the drowned corpse is three feet long, twenty-two pounds, and has many external features similar to a large rat. But its face is a distended and warped human face. Its teeth have mercury gold amalgam fillings popular from the later 19th century, the kind replaced in the last thirty years by composites.

The cover-up is easy enough. Pensions are dangled. The cops and animal-control guys just shrug and walk away. It's New York. Not their problem.

"You think we got them all?"

We'll see. Now, the team gone home, I sit in the hotel watching Home Hunters, eating take out, waiting for the call. Every once and a while I look at the phone and think, "How many of those things would it take to move a fourteen-pound baby?" I think, "Could it speak?" I think, "What was its name?"

How did it become this...thing?

Dozens of human eyes looking back.

I try not to think.

He Dies, Again

THE THREE-HUNDREDTH-SOMETHING TIME THROUGH, he
dies, again.

To avoid the accident on 12th Street, I always end up on
Telegraph heading towards Demont. Sometimes it's 2:46 A.M.
Sometimes it's 2:44 A.M. Once, in an amazing confluence of
events, it was 2:22 A.M. I still don't know how that happened.
I've never gotten it to happen again. Still, it gives me hope. I'm
in a loop, yes, but there are shortcuts. I'm trying to brute-force
collapse the wave-form to its most efficient structure.

I read the report on the machine.

Maybe there's even a way out. If I can make the machine
before we turn it on, I can close it down. So far, the closest I've
come is to stand two hundred yards from the facility when the
power suddenly blooms. Then, a moment later, I'm at the start.

The start is always the same. Everyone who was in the
room near the machine is in a field of junked cars and waist-
high reeds in winter, 21.3 miles from the lab. Agent Darrow
is obviously dead. Agent Denton is breathing her last, burned
across most of her body. And there I am, untouched, legs tingly
and buried a quarter of an inch into the mud.

Usually, I pull out of the mud and start to run immediately.
At first, I went towards the lights. Now I know that's the wrong
way. The white car is double-parked, idling on Thomas Street,
while the driver tries to lock a gate across a fifty-yard dirt-cov-
ered field. And I'm always gone before I even hear what he has

to say to me. Though I always see his shadow in the rear-view as I drive off.

I've tried other things, of course.

I've tried to ditch and go on foot (the two hundred and twenty-fifth time through). That didn't work. I never make it to the device in time. I've stolen cars. I've crossed rooftops. Once, I ran barefoot holding a pistol and screaming until I collapsed before the loop closed again.

But here I am.

The traffic stop. Jesus. I don't even count anymore. I can't count.

He comes to the car and taps on the glass, and I roll down the window. His name is Edgar Lustayre, Jr. The twentieth time I shot him, I stumbled across to the print shop, shot the plexiglass door out, and looked him up with his ID folded open on the desk. That was, I don't know, a month ago. A year?

There was a lot of blood. It's OK. It goes away with the re-set. That reset happened about five minutes after they shot the tear gas in. My eyes were still watering the next time through.

But enough about me. Lustayre.

He grew up in Grant Park, Idaho. He was on the football team in high school. He went to Northwestern. He dropped out and became a cop.

Another time through, I called in a favor.

"Hey, Mark, can you get me a file on a...uh...Officer Edgar Lustayre, Jr., Greenville Police, SSN 079-71-5382."

If he could see me now. Cut up. Messed up. A murderer.

A murderer a hundred times over. At least. I once killed ten people in one go. Just shot everyone I saw. Until the world restored itself. It's OK. It's not real.

"Jesus, Bobby, what time is it?"

"Come on, Mark. It's important."

"Fine."

Lustaryre, Jr., is clean. No record. Not a blemish. A clean cop. He has a kid. A wife. What was I looking for? An excuse? Something to make me feel better.

Anyway, I kill him, again.

Each time it's a little different.

"Sir, do you..."

This time, I roll down the window, and I shoot him immediately from the hip. Right in the face. A flat pop and a pencil-eraser-sized hole in his upper lip. The wet sound of something on the ground, and he drops like someone clipped his strings. I'm sorry, Mr....Officer Lustayre. I'm sorry, dude.

I peel out.

There's more, of course. The dog I almost always hit. Hell, I try to hit him this time. The train. The weird lights on Macgrath Street.

This time, something feels right.

I run down the fence, straight through it. I can see or sense the security guards from the booth running towards me. I know their names. Where they live. I know the fat one went to a wedding last weekend. It was on his Facebook page. I know too much. So much, it feels like it's spilling out of my eyes and into the world.

The sign on the building swings into view through
a spidered windshield: MARCH TECHNOLOGIES. I
hear shouting.

I hop from the vehicle at speed and stumble into a dead
run. Someone is shooting at me, I think. I don't look at the
time. Time is on my side. I don't look.

I have my keycard, and I open the doors. One. Two. Three.
What time is it? What's the time?

And I throw the door open to Lab 2A, and I see...me.
Denton is messing with the machine. Darrow turns to see me
see myself. I begin walking towards me. I pull my gun and draw
a bead on Denton.

"What the fuck?" I say to myself.

I raise the gun at Denton, but I am in the way. I have to
shoot Denton.

I stop me. I run and tackle me, and we land in the doorway.

"No. No. No," I think I'm saying.

In the shielded door, sprawled, our view of the machine
and Denton is obscured, when the loop resets.

Mud. A darkened field. Denton breathing her last. But
there's something new. I'm holding someone. I look into my
face and see my expression go from fear to confusion. I smile.
It's different. It's changed. It's different.

There are two of me.

"LISTEN. It's already too late for us on this run. But we
can change this."

Awake

I WRITE IT ALL down, but the words that wait for me when I pick my journal (so real: leather, smells of coffee, with a red bookmark) remain gibberish. They are not that way when I write them down. The words feel so real. Almost as if they are the only real thing here. But the language runs like wet paint, and I cannot recall what I put down there the time before. I do remember that the last place I sat and wrote was warm, with the smell of cinnamon and the feeling of a fire burning somewhere in a cold house. But I can't recall where that was, or when exactly, except it was before. At some point, the armies came. As the shelling began, I picked up my belongings (did my journal have a blue bookmark?) and left in the dead of a summer's night. Listening as the crickets droned, pausing after each distant shell blast, walking the night road.

Something wouldn't let me see the house I had come from, but I could see across the night-lit vale, past the shadows of trees, to distant, pulsing lights. Booms that carried across the world like the words of God. I think I stood and watched the sorties for a bit.

Now I wake in a rainy field and I still can't shake the feeling of exhaustion. The sky is low and close and gray, but somehow still bright. I open my journal, and it loads quickly—showing, surprisingly, the date, June 18—and the cursor blinks. I type as fast as I can, without thinking, and then review. I slept at a farmhouse and wandered off at the height of summer only to wake in a field in the middle of what feels like October. For a moment, something very clear rises in my mind. A vision.

A woman stands in my view, holding an odd crown. It is metal, with tines of copper wires running from it, and the portion that will touch my skin (is touching my skin?) is set with tiny beads of rubber. I can see a piece of masking tape on the inside of the crown. Writing there says, "Left lead occipital." The woman smiles, and her front right tooth is discolored as if it had died some time before.

"Michael?" she says. She seems familiar in some odd way, though I'm sure I don't know her. "Are you ready?"

"Ready," I say.

The vision fades. I write this down too, breaking the narrative. And what does it matter? Tomorrow, the journal will be gibberish, anyway.

Now, just the field. The grass ripples with the wind in curls, looping away from me in fractal patterns. A drizzle of cold water sprays me with each wind blast, but the feeling isn't one of discomfort. It's of waking up.

I feel very cold. This feeling rises in me until I have to close the journal and stand up. I pocket the journal and cap my pen and slip it in my pocket, and look around. The field is green and cold. The rain begins in earnest. Then, I see it.

Across the field, perhaps a half mile distant, an irregular object. Though I don't know why I'm excited, I run towards it. It warms me, the run. I feel wet and cold and overheated at the same time. When I arrive, I lay my hand on it before I even register what it is.

It's a steel cabinet, as tall as me, standing in the middle of the field. It rocks a little when I lean on it. A sticker on the front says NUKE THE WHALES. That seems familiar. Then I see, twenty-five feet from it, a tipped-over chair. I jog over to it. I pull it up from the wet grass as the wind roars in my ears and the sky completely opens up. Rain is pouring down.

Further on, through the torrential rain, a metal hospital bed in the field.

Copper wires cluster and run in odd half-loops towards the bed. As I get closer, I can hear people—distantly—shouting. "It's time to wake up now, John." "Hello! Hello!" "Wake up now, John! Wake up!"

A man is in the bed.

I get five steps towards it and then stop. The rain is roaring. The wind whips it in my eyes, and I keep wiping them, looking at the figure in the bed, nothing more than a blurred lump under a white cover.

I turn and run away from the bed. First, the rain slows and then stops. The wind dies down. And finally, when I cross into the trees, the air seems to bloom with sudden heat. Bugs flit in the air, and finally, sunlight dapples down through the canopy, lighting my way.

I feel good. I feel awake again. Finally.

The First Report

When Chilton took his shot, I jumped into the mirror room with the laptop bag thinking, anywhere is better than here. Right at that moment, it seemed like a good play. Guns were out and people were already dead. What did I have to lose?

Don't answer yet.

The old McTeague luck is holding up great, pops. Trust me, you'd be proud.

From the lab at San Francisco University, the mirror room inexplicably opened onto a shallow sea beneath a wall of diamond-hard pinpoints of light. I goggled and stumbled and laughed. I don't know why. It was so surprising, I guess. The water was tropic, the low rock islands steaming, and I could taste metal in my mouth. Then the mirror room folded in on itself like origami. It felt like someone had grabbed both sides of my brain and was twisting them, pulling them apart.

Before it was gone, I was gone.

I woke with my head in the mud, soaked in warm water, the lone occupant of this place. World. I stood. I shouted. Knee-deep clear water, low rock islands. Nothing. No mirrors. No people. No life. When I breathed too fast, I began to feel happy and stupid. The computer was shorted out in the water, but there was some damp paper. A pen. Some M&Ms.

I sat for a time trying to catch up with what the world had become, for me. I took off my shoes and soaked my feet.

Then, one last indignity. The moon rose, crazy close. Huge and unblemished as the face of a child. Its surface white and perfect and empty, like the eons and epochs ahead that will toil on without me, forward, until my birth comes around again.

I'll write my last report here. Hell, the first report. I'll write the first one. I am the first agent, now. It's all I have, so don't deny it to me. OK?

Hello?

Dear V-cell,

Do not enter the mirror room. Do not let John enter the mirror room. Destroy the mirror room. Destroy Auroratech. Destroy John. Destroy the world. Dear V-cell, nothing is real, and everything is alive. The end has come and will come and come again.

Find my bones here and see. Know. Wait for me. I'm coming. But time moves so slowly.

About the Author

DENNIS DETWILLER IS AN author, artist and video game de-
signer. Since 1992, his books, card games and video games have
entertained over 40 million people in 11 languages. In a 15-year
video-game career he produced best-selling mobile and console games for Warner Bros. International Enterprises, Hare-
brained Schemes, Nickelodeon, Hothead Games, and Radical
Entertainment. His work spans global hits such as *Magic: The
Gathering*, the *[PROTOTYPE]* series for Activision, *Teenage
Mutant Ninja Turtles* for Nickelodeon, and more personal
creations such as *Delta Green, GODLIKE* and *Wild Talents*.
He contributed to the #1 collectible card game in the world
(Magic: The Gathering) and produced the #1 console game
([PROTOTYPE], 2009) and the #1 iOS game *(Teenage Mutant
Ninja Turtles: Rooftop Run,* 2013). He has won many Origins
Awards and Ennie Awards for RPG excellence. Read more
of his fiction in *Delta Green: Tales From Failed Anatomies,
Delta Green: Extraordinary Renditions, Delta Green: Through
a Glass, Darkly* (a sequel to John Scott Tynes' *The Rules of
Engagement,* found in *Delta Green: Strange Authorities)* and
Delta Green: Denied to the Enemy.

About Delta Green

DELTA GREEN BEGAN, UNDER another name, as a U.S. Navy program to investigate the terrifying implications of the federal government's little-known 1928 raid on Innsmouth, Massachusetts. In World War II, that program was folded into an OSS psychological warfare unit dedicated to exploiting Nazi belief in the supernatural — but which really fought to thwart the terrifying supernatural things that certain Nazi researchers had uncovered. Its activities were classified DELTA GREEN.

After the war, Delta Green split apart. Many of its veterans joined a new program, code-named MAJESTIC, after the Roswell incident revealed what appeared to be UFOs and alien life — discoveries which concealed a far more horrifying truth. What remained of Delta Green pursued supernatural threats across the globe for decades, until a disastrous Cambodia operation in 1970 shut the group down.

Delta Green never really went away. Its leaders went underground, pulling strings from within the U.S government to send hand-picked agents on new operations. They kept fighting to uproot and destroy supernatural terrors just as they had been fighting since Innsmouth, despite the awful toll they paid in life and sanity.

In 2001, Delta Green agents staged a sort of coup in the MAJESTIC program, a very hostile takeover that split Delta Green apart again. With the onset of the Global War on Terror, the Defense Department's long-defunct DELTA GREEN classification was reactivated for a top-secret, highly restricted program, fighting cosmic terrors with the tools and aegis of the War on Terror. Many Delta Green agents joined the new organization. Others distrusted the close ties between the new Delta Green and the infamously corrupt sprawl of the MAJESTIC program. Those few cut all ties with their former comrades and remained out in the cold, pursuing their desperate work with even fewer resources and less hope than before.

For more information and Delta Green books and games, visit www.delta-green.com.

99054810R00043

Made in the USA
Columbia, SC
08 July 2018